This book belongs to:

Digital art by Callaway Animation Studios under the direction of David Kirk
in collaboration with Nelvana Limited.

Nicholas Callaway, President and Publisher
Cathy Ferrara, Managing Editor and Production Director
Toshiya Masuda, Art Director • Nelson Gomez, Director of Digital Services
Joya Rajadhyaksha, Associate Editor • Amy Cloud, Associate Editor
Krupa Jhaveri, Designer

Special thanks to the Nelvana staff, including Doug Murphy, Scott Dyer, Tracy Ewing, Pam Lehn,
Tonya Lindo, Mark Picard, Jane Sobol, Luis Lopez, Eric Pentz, and Georgina Robinson.

Distributed in the United States by Penguin Young Readers Group.

Callaway Arts & Entertainment, its Callaway logotype,
and Callaway & Kirk Company LLC are trademarks.

ISBN 978-0-448-45006-3

Visit Callaway Arts & Entertainment at www.callaway.com.

10 9 8 7 6 5 4 3 2 1   08 09 10

Printed in China

Miss Spider's
SUNNY PATCH FRIENDS

Welcome to
Sunny Patch

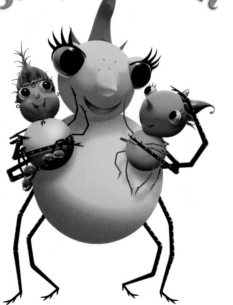

David Kirk

CALLAWAY

NEW YORK

2008

W elcome to Sunny Patch—
where happiness grows!

I am Miss Spider.
I live here with my family in
the Cozy Hole of a big tree.

Holley is my husband.
He loves to play the guitar.

My son Squirt is six. He surfs his web all over Sunny Patch.

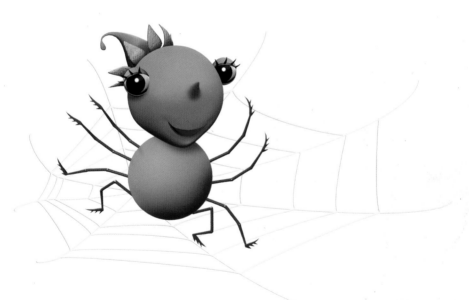

Pansy and Snowdrop are twins.
They like to sing together.

Wiggle paints beautiful
pictures for everybuggy to see.

Shimmer is a star
soccerberry player.

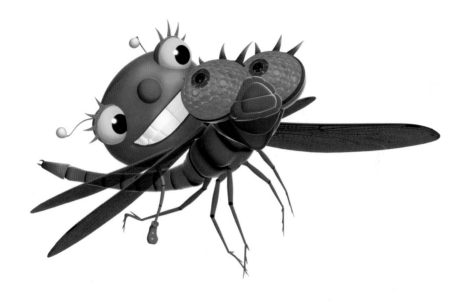

Bounce and Dragon
are best bug buddies.

And Spinner loves to play music.
Do the buggie boogie with us!

In Sunny Patch, we are good to bugs of all shapes, sizes, and colors.

We're good to nature, too—
flowers, trees, plants,
and leaves.

We try to always be kind
to each other.

Sharing shows how much
we care.

Everything is more fun when we are doing it together!